LITTLE MISS PRINCESS
and the Pea

Roger Hargreaves

Original concept by
Roger Hargreaves

Written and illustrated by
Adam Hargreaves

EGMONT

Late one night last week, on her way home Little Miss Princess got caught in a terrible storm and her coach got stuck in the mud.

She saw a light in the distance and decided to seek help and a bed for the night.

She walked through the wind and rain and lightning to the house.

On the way she lost her crown.

Little Miss Princess arrived at the huge house exhausted and looking very wet and bedraggled.

In fact not looking like a Princess at all.

She knocked on the tall front doors.

It was Mr Uppity's house. Mr Uppity is the richest man in the World. He is also one of the rudest men in the World.

"What do you want?" he demanded, rudely, when he opened the door.

Little Miss Princess explained what had happened and asked for a bed for the night.

"You're not coming in here!" he bellowed. "You'll ruin my expensive rugs!"

"Please can you help me," begged Little Miss Princess. "I'm so cold and tired and I just need a bed for the night."

"Go round to the back and I'll see what I can do," he said crossly. With which he slammed the door in her face.

What a rude man!

Mr Uppity led Little Miss Princess into his enormous dining room. The dining table was vast and seated round it were some guests.

Mr Uppity explained the situation to his guests and asked for their suggestions.

"Princesses are really good at dancing. Let's dance!" suggested Mr Bump.

And of course Mr Bump trod on her toes and sent her flying across the floor.

"Hopeless!" cried Mr Uppity. "Can't dance, so she can't possibly be a Princess!"

"Princesses are really good at waving," said Mr Tickle.

Now, Little Miss Princess was very proud of her waving and loved to wave to people from her coach, but every time she raised her arm Mr Tickle tickled her.

He tickled her so much she fell over on the floor.

"Can't wave, can't dance and look at her, on the floor again!" said Mr Uppity, impatiently. "Decidedly not a Princess!"

"I have heard," piped up Little Miss Splendid, "that Princesses are very delicate. So delicate that if they sleep with even a pea under their mattress they will wake in the morning bruised all over."

"Mmmm," said Mr Uppity. "That's an interesting idea."

So Mr Uppity went off to find a pea and the others all trooped upstairs.

Mr Mean lifted the mattress and Mr Uppity placed the pea underneath.

Mr Mean looked at the bed. "Not much of a test," he said.

"Quite right, Mr Mean. More mattresses!" he ordered.

So they piled mattress after mattress, one on top of the other, until they nearly reached the ceiling.

And then Little Miss Princess climbed on top.

"Good night," said Mr Uppity, and he turned out the light.

And then Mr Uppity went to bed.

Although not the sort of bed he had hoped for.

There was not a bed in the house left with a mattress on it.

Mr Uppity was up very early the next day. Partly to see how the test had worked, but also because he had had a dreadful night's sleep.

"How did you sleep?" Mr Uppity asked Little Miss Princess.

"I had a wonderful night's sleep," she replied.

"Ah!" cried Mr Uppity. "I knew you weren't a Princess!"

"And yet, I still got to sleep in your biggest and most comfortable bed!" beamed Little Miss Princess.

"Oh," said a suddenly crestfallen Mr Uppity.

Poor Little Miss Princess had to trudge all the way round the house. Mr Uppity opened the back door.

"Took your time! You can sleep in there," he said, pointing to a cold, damp cellar.

"But I'm a Princess!" spluttered Little Miss Princess.

"You don't look like one!" snapped Mr Uppity. "You don't even have a crown."

"I lost it in the storm," explained Little Miss Princess.

"A likely story," said Mr Uppity. "If you are a Princess then you will have to prove it!"

"And if you are going to test for Princesses in the future," she added, "you should use an uncooked pea, not a cooked one."

With which she lifted the mattresses and revealed a squashed pea!

Mr Uppity went very red in the face and did not know what to say, he was so embarrassed.

And Little Miss Princess went home.

"A waste of a good pea, if you ask me," muttered Mr Mean.